WHALE ALERT!

Tybee Craddock and the Endangered Right Whale

by Emily Slusher & Angela Kakabeeke

Illustrated by Tara Garrigan

Blue, Green & Clean

EARTH DETECTIVES™

ISBN 978-0-9906665-4-7

Dedicated to Earth Detectives:
Cooper, Hazel, Hudson, Claire, Zane, Tucker, G and all those in search of things
Blue, Green and Clean.

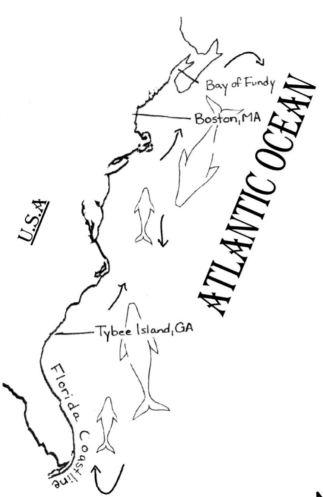

U.S.A

Bay of Fundy

Boston, MA

ATLANTIC OCEAN

Tybee Island, GA

Florida Coastline

N
W   E
S

Seasonal Migratory Path
of the
North Atlantic Right Whale

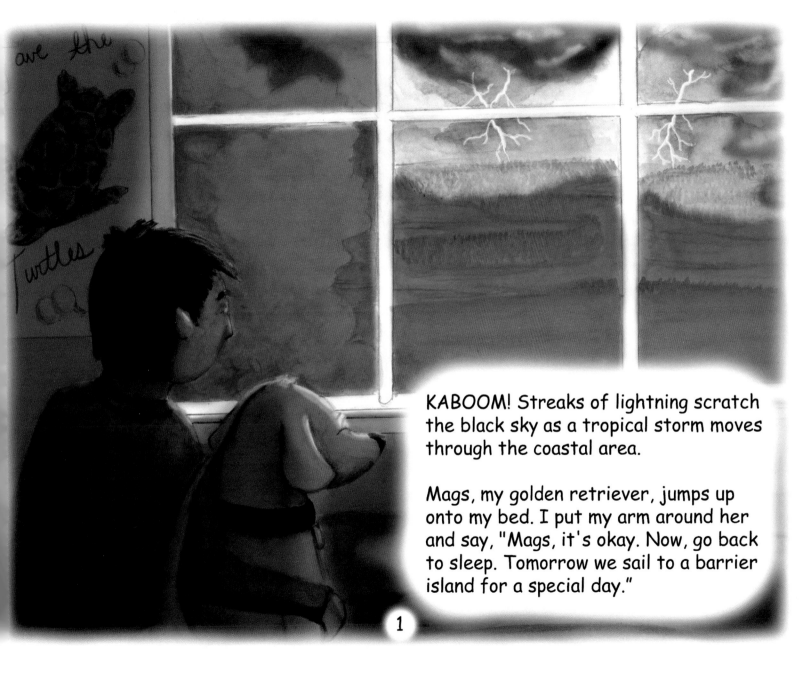

KABOOM! Streaks of lightning scratch the black sky as a tropical storm moves through the coastal area.

Mags, my golden retriever, jumps up onto my bed. I put my arm around her and say, "Mags, it's okay. Now, go back to sleep. Tomorrow we sail to a barrier island for a special day."

1

I'm first to the kitchen table.
Mom gives me a hug and says,
"Good morning, Tybee Craddock!"

Just as the family joins hands expressing thanks for the food, our cyber watchphones "BEEP" with a Whale Alert!

Sailing past the lighthouse, I scan the area looking for the right whales with my binoculars.

7

Steering past Pier 51, we head towards the barrier island. Again, I look through my binoculars. "What's that I see?"

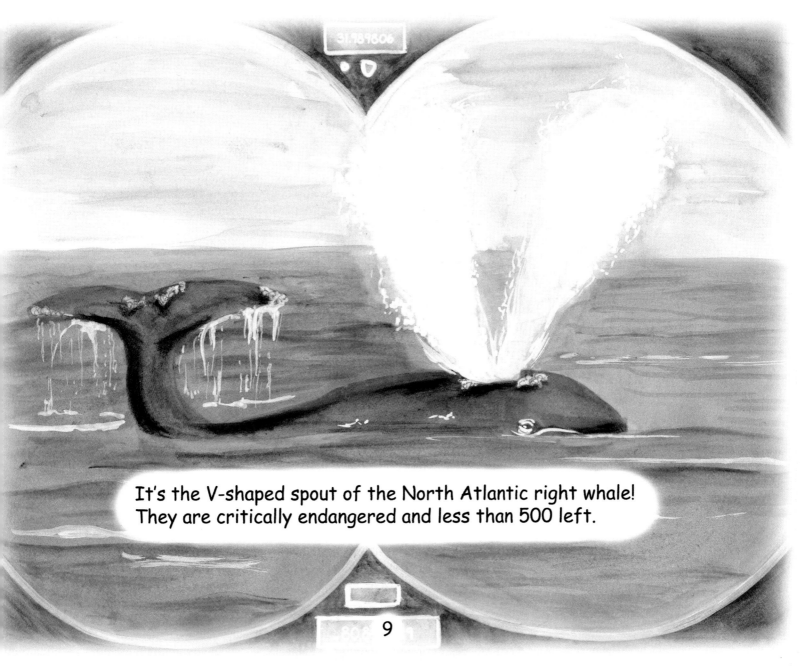

Little Dipper

North Star
(Polaris)

Home of Little Man

Big Dipper

"Little Man, Little Man, come quickly, please!

"Little Man, help us solve this mystery."

12

Faster than a thunderbolt, Little Man appears in a teeny-tiny helicopter. He is dressed in a teeny-tiny pilot's jumpsuit with a teeny-tiny helmet and goggles.

I tell him about the mystery of the right whale's spout. He gets back in his helicopter and lifts off.

13

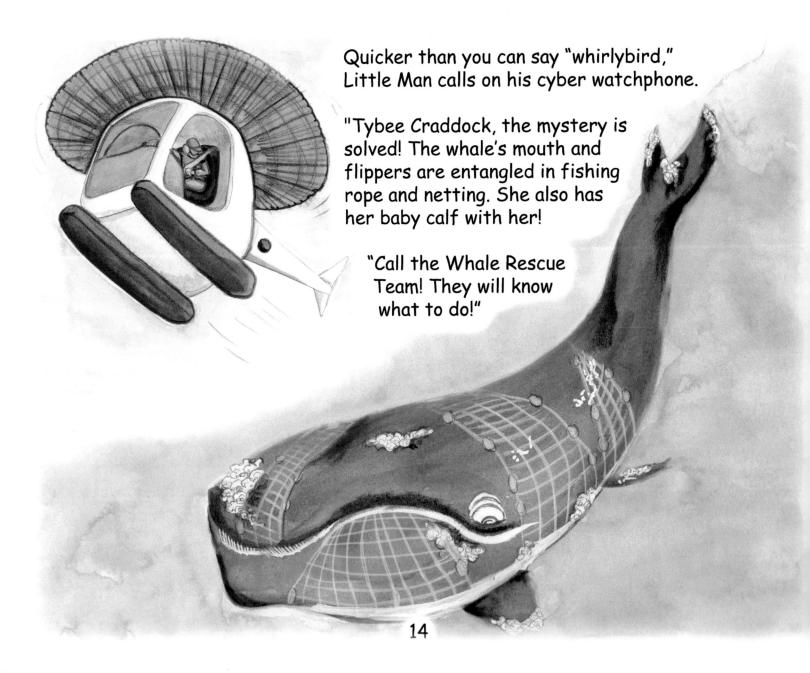

Quicker than you can say "whirlybird," Little Man calls on his cyber watchphone.

"Tybee Craddock, the mystery is solved! The whale's mouth and flippers are entangled in fishing rope and netting. She also has her baby calf with her!

"Call the Whale Rescue Team! They will know what to do!"

I call them on my cyber watchphone. They ask how I know about the whale.

I tell them a man in a helicopter told me. (Now, I do not say how big he is, because, you see, only kids and dogs can see Little Man.)

They tell me that Dr. Fondue and the rescue team are on their way!

I say, "Thank you, ma'am."

Suddenly. . .

16

The right whale is heading straight towards our sailboat!

Whew! She makes a sharp turn! Now I see what Little Man saw. Her body is entangled in fishing rope and netting!

17

Shortly, the rescue team arrives in their skiff. Whale rescues are a complicated and dangerous operation.

Just so you know, Dr. Fondue uses a specially designed cutting tool. The tool only cuts the fishing rope, but does not harm the whale.

The ropes are cut! We are all wildly excited to see that she is free and with her baby calf. Relieved, we sail on to the barrier island.

"The ocean provides habitats for right whales and other marine life. However, there are manmade hazards in the ocean like fishing rope and netting that entangles them.

"Each one of us can be Earth Detectives and search for ways to keep the earth Blue, Green & Clean. Together, we can make it better for all marine life to swim safely in their home, the sea."

Just then . . .

21

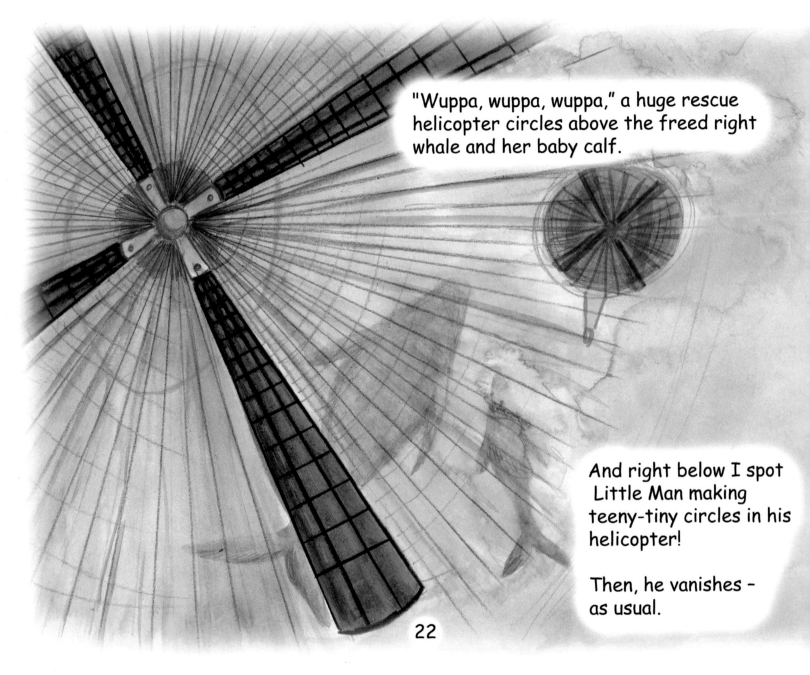

"Wuppa, wuppa, wuppa," a huge rescue helicopter circles above the freed right whale and her baby calf.

And right below I spot Little Man making teeny-tiny circles in his helicopter!

Then, he vanishes – as usual.

The rescue helicopter lands on the beach.
They appreciate my help so much that Mags,
Savannah and I get to ride in the helicopter.
We have a perfect view of the right whale
and her baby calf! "Woohoo!"

... set sail landward to home.

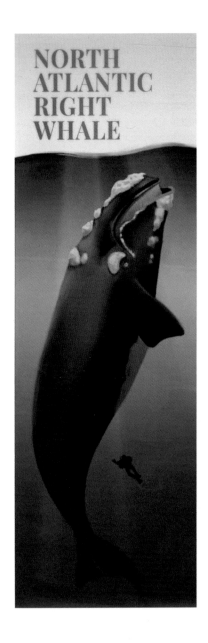

NORTH ATLANTIC RIGHT WHALE

Deep Blue Sea Thinking

1. Right whales have their own name and family. As an example, Phoenix is the name of a famous right whale. Her mother's name is Stumpy. Locate names of other right whales. Share what you have learned.

2. The North Atlantic right whale migrates from the Bay of Fundy down to the Coastal waters of Georgia and Florida at different seasons. Investigate two reasons for migration.

3. A mature right whale grows up to 55 feet long! That's about as long as a school bus. See how long a right whale is by using a string.

4. In the story, Dr. Fondue is a marine biologist. Research and identify what do marine biologist do for their job. What other types of occupations are associated with the study of marine environments?

5. Take action! Send an email to your congressman to pass legislation that will protect the right whale and other marine life.

Resources: *Georgia Department of Natural Resources, Gray's Reef, Tybee Island Marine Science Center, New England Aquarium, NOAA, Sea to Shore Alliance*

Earth Detectives!
Search and Find Pictures in the Story

 ✓ **Fishing rope and netting** - lead core rope and netting used in commercial fishing that can entangle the North Atlantic right whale

 ✓ **Wind Turbines** - devices that converts the wind's kinetic energy into electrical power

 ✓ **Solar Panels** - panels designed to absorb the sun's rays as a source of energy

 ✓ **Monofilament Recycling** - collection bin for fishing line

 ✓ **Marine Biologist** - someone who studies oceans, ocean life and environmental conditions that affect them

 ✓ **International Ocean Clean-Up** - world's largest volunteer effort that occurs every September

Angela on the New England Coast

Emily at Tybee Island

Authors

Angela Kakabeeke and Emily Slusher are Earth Detectives searching for real-life solutions that show care for air, land, and seas. They enjoy discovering actions that individuals, communities, corporations and governments take to help the earth be Blue, Green & Clean.

Angela and Emily live on opposite sides of the USA. However, their paths occasionally intersect and they observe the wonders of nature in: the desert of Arizona, mountains of Colorado, hills of Tennessee, Appalachian Mountains of North Carolina, coastal Georgia, or harbors in Massachusetts. Whether at home or at work, near mountains or seas, they hope to encourage and inspire all to reshape their views and actions in helping the earth be Blue, Green & Clean!

Tara flying over Coastal Georgia

Illustrator

Tara Garrigan lives in Savannah, Georgia where she continues to work as a freelance artist and as part of the production team of Impeller Studios. She enjoys contributing to art education by continuing to teach as much as she can. In her free time, Tara is learning to fly! If you ever get to join her on one of her journeys at 3,000 feet up, you may just be able to watch the migration of the right whales up and down the East Coast, just like Tybee and Savannah.